ASTERIX AND THE GREAT CROSSING

TEXT BY GOSCINNY

DRAWINGS BY UDERZO

TRANSLATED BY ANTHEA BELL AND DEREK HOCKRIDGE

HODDER DARGAUD
LONDON SYDNEY AUCKLAND

ASTERIX IN OTHER COUNTRIES

Australia	Hodder Dargaud, 2 Apollo Place, Lane Cove, New South Wales 2066, Australia
Austria	Delta Verlag, Postfach 1215, 7 Stuttgart 1, West Germany
Belgium	Dargaud Bénélux, 3 rue Kindermans, 1050 Brussels, Belgium
Brazil	Record Distribuidora, Rua Argentina 171, 20921 Rio de Janeiro, Brazil
Canada	Dargaud Canada, 307 Benjamin Hudon, St Laurent, Montreal H4N 1J1, Canada
Denmark	Serieforlaget A/S (Gutenberghus Group), Vognmagergade 11, 1148 Copenhagen K, Denmark
Esperanto	Delta Verlag, Postfach 1215, 7 Stuttgart 1, West Germany
Finland	Sanoma Corporation, P.O. Box 107, 00381 Helsinki 38, Finland
France	Dargaud Editeur, 12 Rue Blaise Pascal, 92201 Neuilly sur Seine, France
	(titles up to and including Asterix in Belgium)
	Les Editions Albert René, 81 Avenue Marceau, 75116 Paris, France
	(titles from Asterix and the Great Divide, onwards)
Germany, West	Delta Verlag, Postfach 1215, 7 Stuttgart 1, West Germany
Holland	Dargaud Bénélux, 3 rue Kindermans, 1050 Brussels, Belgium
	(Distribution) Van Ditmar b.v., Oostelijke Handelskade 11, 1019 BL, Amsterdam, Holland
Hong Kong	Hodder Dargaud, c/o United Publishers Book Services, Stanhope House, 13th Floor, 734 King's Road, Hong Kong
Hungary	Nip Forum, Vojvode Misica 1-3, 2100 Novi Sad, Yugoslavia
India	*(Hindi)* Gowarsons Publishers Private Ltd, Gulab House, Mayapuri, New Delhi 110 064, India
Indonesia	Penerbit Sinar Harapan, J1. Dewi Sartika 136D, Jakarta Cawang, Indonesia
Israel	Dahlia Pelled Publishers, 5 Hamekoubalim St, Herzeliah 46447, Israel
Italy	Dargaud Italia, Via M. Buonarroti 38, 20145 Milan, Italy
Latin America	Grijalbo-Dargaud S.A., Deu y Mata 98-102, Barcelona 29, Spain
New Zealand	Hodder Dargaud, P.O. Box 3858, Auckland 1, New Zealand
Norway	A/S Hjemmet (Gutenburghus Group), Kristian den 4des gt 13, Oslo 1, Norway
Portugal	Meriberica, Avenida Alvares Cabral 84-1° Dto, 1296 Lisbon, Portugal
Roman Empire	*(Latin)* Delta Verlag, Postfach 1215, 7 Stuttgart 1, West Germany
Southern Africa	Hodder Dargaud, P.O. Box 548, Bergvlei, Sandton 2012, South Africa
Spain	Grijalbo-Dargaud S.A., Deu y Mata 98-102, Barcelona 29, Spain
Sweden	Hemmets Journal Forlag (Gutenberghus Group), Fack, 200 22 Malmö, Sweden
Switzerland	Interpress Dargaud S.A., En Budron B, 1052 Le Mont/Lausanne, Switzerland
Turkey	Kervan Kitabcilik, Basin Sanayii ve Ticaret AS, Tercuman Tesisleri, Topkapi-Istanbul, Turkey
USA	Dargaud Publishing International Ltd, 2 Lafayette Court, Greenwich, Conn. 06830, USA
Wales	*(Welsh)* Gwasg Y Dref Wen, 28 Church Road, Whitchurch, Cardiff, Wales
Yugoslavia	Nip Forum, Vojvode Misica 1-3, 2100 Novi Sad, Yugoslavia

Asterix and the Great Crossing

ISBN 0 340 20211 4 (cased)
ISBN 0 340 21589 5 (limp)

Copyright © Dargaud Editeur 1975, Goscinny-Uderzo
English language text copyright © Hodder and Stoughton Ltd 1976

First published in Great Britain 1976 (cased)
This impression 1986

First published in Great Britain 1978 (limp)
This impression 1988

Published by Hodder Dargaud Ltd,
Mill Road, Dunton Green, Sevenoaks, Kent TN13 2YJ

Printed in Belgium by Henri Proost et Cie, Turnhout

The year is 50 BC. Gaul is entirely occupied by the Romans. Well, not entirely… One small village of indomitable Gauls still holds out against the invaders. And life is not easy for the Roman legionaries who garrison the fortified camps of Totorum, Aquarium, Laudanum and Compendium…

a few of the Gauls

Asterix, the hero of these adventures. A shrewd, cunning little warrior; all perilous missions are immediately entrusted to him. Asterix gets his superhuman strength from the magic potion brewed by the druid Getafix...

Obelix, Asterix's inseparable friend. A menhir delivery-man by trade; addicted to wild boar. Obelix is always ready to drop everything and go off on a new adventure with Asterix – so long as there's wild boar to eat, and plenty of fighting.

Getafix, the venerable village druid. Gathers mistletoe and brews magic potions. His speciality is the potion which gives the drinker superhuman strength. But Getafix also has other recipes up his sleeve...

Cacofonix, the bard. Opinion is divided as to his musical gifts. Cacofonix thinks he's a genius. Everyone else thinks he's unspeakable. But so long as he doesn't speak, let alone sing, everybody likes him...

Finally, Vitalstatistix, the chief of the tribe. Majestic, brave and hot-tempered, the old warrior is respected by his men and feared by his enemies. Vitalstatistix himself has only one fear; he is afraid the sky may fall on his head tomorrow. But as he always says, 'Tomorrow never comes.'

YOU WAIT AND SEE! YOU'LL ÅLL FIND OUT I'M RIGHT! **ÅND NØW SHUT UP!**

ØVER TØ PØRT JUST Å WHISKER!

I SEE...

(BUT LET US LEAVE THESE ICY SEAS, VEILED IN DENSE, IMPENETRABLE MISTS...)

①

5

6

9

LET'S KEEP CALM, OBELIX. THIS BOAT SEEMS VERY SEAWORTHY; PERHAPS THE WIND WILL HAVE DIED DOWN TOMORROW. GOOD NIGHT.

GOOD NIGHT, ASTERIX! GOOD NIGHT, DOGMATIX!

WOOF!

ZZZZ

ZZZZ

ZZZ...SNIFF?

GRRRRRR!

ASTERIX! DOGMATIX HAS PICKED UP A SCENT!

TELL HIM TO GO TO SLEEP. THERE'S NOTHING AROUND HERE EXCEPT US.

GRRRØØÅÅRRR!

7A

DID YOU HEAR THAT, ASTERIX?

YES...

PERHAPS IT'S A MONSTER! WE'VE COME TO THE EDGE OF THE SEA, WHERE CREATURES FROM THE DEPTHS OF HELL...

TAKE IT EASY, OBELIX!!!

NEAR BY...

BY ÅLL THE GØDS! VØICES! WHÅT HÅVE YØU GØT US INTØ, HERENDETHELESSEN?

STEÅDY, STEPTØÅNSSEN! PERHÅPS IT'S THE SIRENS TRYING TØ LURE US WITH THEIR MELØDIØUS SØNG. LET'S STØP UP ØUR EÅRS!

WE'LL NEVER GET ØUT ØF THIS, HERENDETHELESSEN... HERENDETHELESSEN? HERENDETHELESSEN!!!

WHÅT?

ØH! I THØUGHT YØU'D LEFT.

STØP UP YØUR EÅRS ÅND SHUT UP!!!

BUT EVEN THE DARKEST NIGHTS COME TO AN END, AND THE SUN RISES, FAR AWAY FROM THESE MYSTERIOUS INCIDENTS...

7B

YOU SEE? WE HAVEN'T COME TO THE EDGE OF THE SEA, THERE AREN'T ANY MONSTERS, AND THE WIND'S DIED DOWN.

WE CAN'T SEE LAND ANY MORE...

WE'LL TURN BACK HOME AS SOON AS WE GET A FAVOURABLE BREEZE. WE'VE JUST GOT TO WAIT.

I'M HUNGRY!

THINK OF SOMETHING ELSE.

IF YOU HADN'T TOLD ME TO THROW OUT THE NET, WE COULD HAVE CAUGHT SOME FISH... I'D RATHER EAT A BOAR, OF COURSE.

I SAID THINK OF SOMETHING ELSE... THINK OF YOUR MENHIRS.

WITH THAT SAUCE IMPEDIMENTA MAKES, I COULD EAT A MENHIR... REMEMBER THAT SAUCE?

MMM, YES!... VERY GOOD, SPECIALLY WHEN SHE PUTS IN THOSE LITTLE ONIONS AND BITS OF BACON...

ASTERIX! I'M HUNGRY!

I'M HUNGRY TOO! IT'S YOU MAKING ME HUNGRY, GOING ON ABOUT MENHIRS WITH ONIONS!

?

GRRRRR...

LOOK!

A SHIP!

WELL, WELL, WELL! IT'S OUR OLD FRIENDS!

SHALL WE GET THEM? SHALL WE GET THEM?

JUST A MOMENT. HOW ABOUT A CHANGE IN THE SCRIPT? IT'S MY BIRTHDAY TODAY... YOU WOULDN'T WANT TO SPOIL MY BIRTHDAY, WOULD YOU? JUST TELL ME WHAT YOU WANT AND THEN GO AWAY THIS ONCE WITHOUT SINKING ANYTHING.

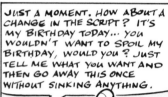

OH, WE'RE ONLY LOOKING FOR A BITE TO EAT!

ASTERIX! LOOK WHAT I'VE FOUND!

WE DON'T WANT TO BE TOO GREEDY; WE'LL LEAVE YOU THIS SAUSAGE. HAPPY BIRTHDAY!

SOON AFTERWARDS...

HAPPY BIRTHDAY TO YOU, HAPPY BIRTHDAY TO YOU...

ALL RIGHT, DON'T OVERDO IT!

CHOP! CHOP!

14

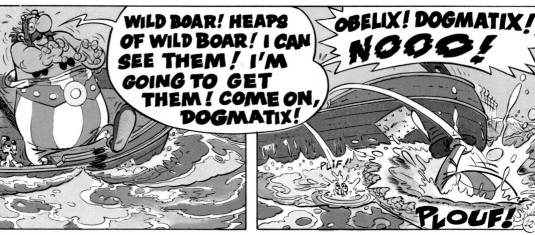

GOBBLE GOBBLE GOBBLE

HOWWWL!

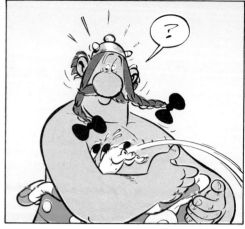

?

FUNNY SORT OF CREATURE!

LET'S FIND OUT WHAT IT TASTES LIKE. I'LL CATCH IT WHILE YOU LIGHT THE FIRE!

HEY, ASTERIX!

THAT GOBBLER HAS LOTS OF FRIENDS. WE'LL HAVE SOMETHING TO EAT WHILE WE WAIT FOR THE BOARS TO TURN UP.

GRRR! WOOF!

LET'S HOPE IT'S EDIBLE.

SOON AFTERWARDS...

IT'S GOOD!

YES, BUT IT MIGHT BE EVEN BETTER STUFFED... SCRUNCH! ... WITH BOAR, FOR INSTANCE...

SCRUNCH! SCRUNCH!

GRRRR!

TALK OF THE DEVIL ... THERE MUST BE A BOAR OVER THERE. I'LL GO AFTER IT. WE CAN USE IT TO STUFF THE THIRD GOBBLER.

BE CAREFUL!

JUST LOOK AT THIS!

???

11

THE BATTLE IS SHORT, OWING TO THE CLEVER MANOEUVRES CARRIED OUT BY THE LEGIONARIES, NOTABLY A SKILFUL WITHDRAWAL TOWARDS PREVIOUSLY PREPARED POSITIONS...

FOR A FEW OF THEM, HOWEVER, THERE WAS NOT ENOUGH TIME TO MANOEUVRE...

WHAT WAS THAT?

THAT WAS A WORD OUT OF PLACE!

MEANWHILE...

THE ROMANS REALLY WANT THIS CHILD! I WISH I KNEW WHY!

YOU'D LIKE TO KNOW THE REASON WHY WE'RE FIGHTING TOO, WOULD YOU, CHIEF?

WELL, SONNY? TELL US WHAT BROUGHT YOU FROM HISPANIA TO GAUL.

10A

MY DADDY IS THE STRONGEST DADDY IN THE WORLD AND SILLY OLD JULIUS CAESAR IS FRIGHTENED OF MY DADDY AND SILLY OLD JULIUS CAESAR HAD ME BROUGHT TO GAUL TO FRIGHTEN MY DADDY BUT THAT WON'T STOP MY DADDY BASHING SILLY OLD JULIUS CAESAR.

OLÉ!

A HOSTAGE! HE'S A HOSTAGE! WE MUST PROTECT HIM FROM THE ROMANS. HE MUST NOT LEAVE THE VILLAGE!

OBELIX! I'M HANDING THIS LITTLE TERROR OVER TO YOU. AND DON'T FORGET THAT AS YOUR GUEST, HE'S SACRED!

YOU MEAN HE'S A HOLY TERROR?

WHAT'S YOUR FIRST NAME, SON OF A CHIEF?

PERICLES. WE'VE GOT SOME GREEK ANCESTORS. AT HOME THEY CALL ME PEPE.

10B

HOW STUPID OF US! IT'S ALL ALL RIGHT!

BEATI PAUPERES SPIRITU, AND I SHOULD KNOW!

IT COMES TO THE SAME THING WHETHER IT'S US OR THE GAULS WHO LOOK AFTER THE HOSTAGE! ALL WE HAVE TO DO IS MAKE SURE THEY DON'T TAKE HIM ANYWHERE ELSE!

YOU'RE RIGHT! I'LL STATION LOOK-OUT MEN ALL ROUND THE VILLAGE!

THAT'S THE WAY!

AND THE BEST OF IT IS THAT THE GAULS WILL HAVE TO LIVE WITH THE LITTLE MONSTER! SEE HOW THEY LIKE IT!

SURE ENOUGH...

THIS IS A DEAD BORE!

A BOAR – BORING?

THERE ISN'T ANYTHING ELSE, ANYWAY.

VERY WELL! I'M GOING TO HOLD MY BREATH UNTIL THERE IS!

?

ER... SAUSAGES? HAM? BLACK PUDDING? BACON? AQUAE SULIS CHAPS? FISH?

FISH! I WANT FISH!

OBELIX, GO AND BUY SOME FISH.

BUT I HAVEN'T FINISHED MY BOAR! IT'LL GET COLD.

ALL RIGHT, ALL RIGHT, I'M GOING!

PEPE MAY BE A NUISANCE, BUT HE'S BEEN HITTING IT OFF WELL WITH DOGMATIX SINCE THE FIGHT!

PEPE IS A BAD EXAMPLE TO DOGMATIX! HE'S YOUNG AND EASILY LED... SOMETIMES THEY WHISPER TOGETHER AND LOOK AT ME AND GIGGLE...

WE USED TO GET ON WELL TOGETHER, ME AND DOGMATIX, AND NOW...

WAIT A MINUTE! I THINK I'VE GOT IT...

O BARD CACOFONIX, WOULD YOU LIKE TO LOOK AFTER PEPE AT YOUR PLACE?

IF HE'D LIKE TO COME, IT WOULD BE A PLEASURE!

SOON AFTERWARDS...

I SHALL NOW SING YOU SOME LULLABIES TO SEND YOU TO SLEEP!

SURE ENOUGH...

I'M DREAMING OF A WHITE SOLSTICE...

?!

OLÉ! IT REMINDS ME OF HOME, ESPECIALLY THE GOATS! ANOTHER ONE, HOMBRE, ANOTHER ONE!

CLAC.

ROCKABYE, PEPE, ON THE TREE TOP...

YOU KNOW, ASTERIX, I'M BEGINNING TO THINK IT IS OUR MORAL DUTY TO RESTORE THAT CHILD TO ITS PARENTS.

YES, IT'S A QUESTION OF MORALE.

WONDERFUL, WONDERFUL DUROVERNUM...

I CAN'T STAND IT ANY LONGER! BACTERIA! BRING ME A FISH... A BIG ONE!

THE ONE THE CHIEF HIT YOU WITH?

NEXT DAY...

WHERE IS YOUR VILLAGE, PEPE?

I DON'T KNOW WHERE IT IS, BUT IT'S THE BEST VILLAGE IN THE WORLD AND MY HOUSE IS THE BEST HOUSE IN THE VILLAGE AND YOU STILL HAVE A BIG NOSE!

THOSE ARE NOT ADEQUATE DIRECTIONS...

IF HE'S TOO SMALL TO TELL US WHERE HE LIVES, IT'S GOING TO BE TRICKY TAKING HIM BACK HOME.

THE ROMANS KNOW WHERE HE LIVES. WE ONLY HAVE TO ASK THEM.

GOOD IDEA! THEY'VE STATIONED LOOK-OUTS ALL ROUND OUR VILLAGE, SO WE WON'T HAVE FAR TO GO.

SOON AFTERWARDS...

WE MUST CHOOSE TREES WITH PLENTY OF FOLIAGE AND A GOOD VIEW OF THE VILLAGE. THEY'LL PROVIDE THE BEST PICKINGS.

LET'S TRY THIS ONE!

AHA! THIS LOOKS LIKE THE PICK OF THE BUNCH!

TCHRAC

BOOM!

WHERE EXACTLY DOES THE HOSTAGE COME FROM?

HIS VILLAGE IS A LITTLE WAY TO THE SOUTH OF HISPALIS.* CAN I GET BACK UP MY TREE NOW?

* SEVILLE

HEY! ASTERIX!

THEY'RE NOT SO BIG HERE, BUT THERE ARE MORE OF THEM! SHALL WE TRY ANOTHER TREE?

NO, OBELIX. I'VE GOT ALL I NEED TO KNOW. COME ON!

21

HEY!

POC!

TCHRAC!

BOOM!

IT DOESN'T TAKE MUCH TO GET YOU DOWN.

I FEEL READY TO DROP...

OBVIOUSLY THE GAULS HAVE DECIDED TO TAKE THE HOSTAGE BACK HOME.

AND SOMETHING WE SAID MUST HAVE TOLD THEM WHERE HE LIVES...

SO WE'D BETTER NOT MENTION IT TO OUR COMMANDING OFFICER...

THAT'S RIGHT! LET'S GET BACK UP OUR TREES!

WE'RE NOT NUTS!

AND WHILE EVERYONE AT TOTORUM SEEMS HAPPY...

I SHALL SOON BE REJOINING MY GARRISON IN HISPANIA. I'M NOT NEEDED HERE ANY LONGER. THE GAULS KNOW THEY'RE BEING WATCHED. THEY WON'T MAKE ANY MOVE.

YOU CAN TRUST MY MEN! THEY DON'T GO BARKING UP THE WRONG TREE!

...BACK AT ROME, CAESAR'S TRIUMPH IS A HUGE SUCCESS, AND EVEN HIS CAPTIVE AUDIENCE CAN SCARCE FORBEAR TO CHEER...

Capitol! Capitol!

PAFPAFPAFPAF!

AND CAESAR, DELIGHTED BY THE APPLAUSE OF THE CROWD, MAGNANIMOUSLY SETS THE BARBARIAN CHIEFTAIN FREE.

I SUPPOSE IT'S BECAUSE HE'S CLAPPED IN CHAINS.

YES, IT WAS A CHAIN REACTION.

22

LOOK, ASTERIX! HE'S BROUGHT DOGMATIX! WE MUST TURN BACK!

WE CAN'T DO THAT, OBELIX. WE HAVE A FOLLOWING WIND; WE MUST MAKE THE MOST OF IT.

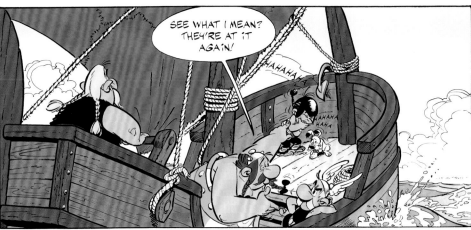

SEE WHAT I MEAN? THEY'RE AT IT AGAIN!

HAHAHA HAHA

A FEW MINUTES LATER...

WHAT DO WE EAT ON THIS VOYAGE, UNHYGIENIX?

FISH, OBELIX. WE'LL CATCH IT AS WE NEED IT.

WE ALWAYS SEEM TO BE ON ABOUT FISH THESE DAYS!

I WANT BOAR!

YOU'LL EAT WHAT'S PUT IN FRONT OF YOU!

HEY! A SAIL!

WE COULD ASK THEM FOR PROVISIONS...

OBELIX, DON'T BE SO PIG-HEADED!

IF WE DON'T, I'M GOING TO HOLD MY BREATH, HOMBRE!

!?!

ALL RIGHT, ALL RIGHT! AFTER ALL, WE REALLY SHOULD HAVE BROUGHT SOMETHING TO EAT... COME ON, UNHYGIENIX, LET'S GO!

ONLY A FISHING BOAT... JUST SMALL FRY. BUT THERE MAY BE A CATCH IN IT.

CAN'T YOU SEE ANYONE WE COULD ATTACK?

HUH! IT'S NOT WORTH BOTHERING WITH. WE'VE JUST TAKEN ON STORES AND WE'RE FULL OF SALT WILD BOAR!

THAT FISHING-BOAT'S ALTERED COURSE! SHE'S BEARING DOWN ON US!!!

AFTER A PLEASANT VOYAGE...

AT LAST...

THE PATH MUST BE OVER THERE, BEHIND THOSE DUNES. YOU CAN EASILY GET INTO HISPANIA THAT WAY.

THANKS! HAVE A NICE JOURNEY HOME, UNHYGIENIX!

GOOD LUCK!

LOOK AT THAT, OBELIX!

HEY, YOU! THIS IS A QUEUE, YOU KNOW! YOU CHAPS IN SPORTS CARTS THINK YOU OWN THE ROAD!

WHAT ARE YOU DOING HERE?

YOU'RE A BIT WET BEHIND THE EARS, AREN'T YOU, BY TOUTATIS? WE'RE ON OUR WAY TO HISPANIA!

WHAT FOR?

FOR OUR HOLIDAY, OF COURSE! THE EXCHANGE RATE IS VERY FAVOURABLE FOR SESTERTII, AND YOU'RE SURE TO FIND THE SUN... I MUST SAY PRICES HAVE RISEN SINCE LAST YEAR. THE NATIVES ARE CATCHING ON...

IT'S SPAINFUL!

TOC! TOC! TOC!

* PAMPLONA

31

WE MUST BE GETTING ON! GOODBYE, AND THANKS!

LATER...

IT'S HOT!

I'M TIRED, ASTERIX!

I'LL ASK THESE TWO LOCALS IF IT'S MUCH FURTHER TO THE TOWN.

NO, IT'S NOT VERY FAR. KEEP RIGHT ON, BEAR LEFT AT THE WINDMILLS...

WINDMILLS? CHARGE!

HEY! HOMBRE! HE'S AT IT AGAIN! WAIT FOR ME!

?

THAT'S POMPAELO OVER THERE... WHAT A LOT OF PEOPLE!

THE TOWN MUST BE ON HOLIDAY.

SURE ENOUGH, THE TOWN IS ON HOLIDAY, AND THE PEOPLE HAVE GATHERED, IN FESTIVE MOOD, TO WATCH THE DRUIDICAL PROCESSION.

33

* SEVILLE

SOON AFTERWARDS...

34

AFTER SEVERAL HOURS' DRIVING...

THERE ARE SOME NOMADS! I LIKE NOMADS, THEY'RE FUNNY. THEY'RE ALWAYS SINGING AND DANCING.

WELL THEN, LET'S STOP AND ASK THEM TO PUT US UP FOR THE NIGHT.

HEY THERE, FRIENDS! COME AND SIT BY THE FIRE AND WE'LL ALL LAUGH AND BE MERRY!

31/A

AYAYAYAYYYYY WOOOOE IS MEEEEE! AYAYAYAYYYYY WHY DID SHEEEEEE LEEEEEEEAVE MEEEEEEEEEE? AYAYAYAYAYAYAYYYYYYYYYY!

CLAPCLAP. CLAP.

OLÉ!
OLÉ!
OLÉ!
OLÉ!
CLAPACLAP! CLAPACLAP.

LET THE MERRYMAKING CONTINUE! NOW FOR SOME DANCING!

OLÉ!

OLÉ!
OLÉ!
CLAPACLAPACLAPACLAPACLAP

TAP, TAP, TAP.

CLAPCLAP!
OLÉ! OLÉ!
CLAPCLAPCLAP!
OLÉ!

OLÉ, GORGEOUS! COME ON, STICK YOUR CHEST OUT!
CLAPACLAP.

I AM! IT'S JUST SLIPPED A BIT!

CLAC.

31B

RIGHT, THEN. OUR MISTAKE... NOW, IF YOU'D BE KIND ENOUGH TO TAKE ONE OF US TO THE NEAREST BREAKDOWN...

FINE! I'LL TAKE THE LITTLE BOY!

NO, WE NEVER LET PEPE OUT OF OUR SIGHT! WE'LL ALL GO, IF IT'S ALL THE SAME TO YOU.

A PLEASURE! OLÉ!

FOILED!

LET'S INTRODUCE OURSELVES. I'M ASTERIX.

I'M OBELIX.

WOOF!

HUEVOS Y BACON!

I'M... ER... I'M OLOROSO EL FIASCO.

SOON AFTERWARDS...

THIS IS WHAT WE WANT.

OFF YOU GO, BOTH OF YOU! PEPE AND I WILL WAIT.

FODDER STATION

CARTS REPAIRED

NO, WE'LL ALL THREE OF US GO WITH PEPE!

OH, ALL RIGHT! I'LL GO ON MY OWN.

LISTEN... THERE ARE SOME PEOPLE OUT THERE WHO NEED A CARTWHEEL. I DON'T WANT YOU TO GIVE THEM A CARTWHEEL. IF THEY COME HERE, JUST TELL THEM YOU HAVEN'T GOT A CARTWHEEL.

!

AND HERE'S SOME MONEY FOR THE CARTWHEEL!

?

!?

BUT HOMBRE, THIS WON'T WORK! I HAVEN'T GOT ANY CARTWHEELS NOT TO GIVE YOU! I'M RIGHT OUT OF STOCK! I'LL HAVE TO ORDER THEM, AND THAT TAKES TIME...

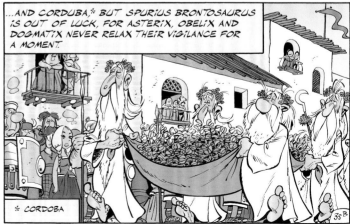

39

NIGHT HAS ALREADY FALLEN WHEN OUR FRIENDS ARRIVE IN HISPALIS, THE CAPITAL OF VANDALUSIA. THE MAGNIFICENT CITY IS FULL OF GAIETY. IT IS A HOLIDAY!

YOU'RE IN LUCK; I'VE GOT TWO ROOMS LEFT, NEXT DOOR TO EACH OTHER.

I'M GOING TO SLEEP IN DOGMATIX'S ROOM.

ME TOO!

ALL RIGHT, THEN, WE'LL SHARE THE OTHER ONE.

SPLENDID! SPLENDID BY JUPI... BY OLE!

DINNER IN THIS TYPICAL VANDALUSIAN INN IS A CHEERFUL OCCASION...

The roads are improving. They're working on them!

A proud and haughty race!

Thin-skinned!

Attractive prices, but they're rising.

They've cottoned on!

The cooking's much better these days.

TODAY'S MENU IS SAUSAGE, SAUERKRAUT AND BEER.

LET'S GO TO BED... WE SAY GOODBYE TOMORROW, MY DEAR AMONTILLADO EL AMOROSO!

OLOROSO EL FIASCO.

GOOD NIGHT.

GOOD NIGHT.

NOW FOR THE MAGIC POTION! THEN I'LL BE THE STRONGEST, AND I CAN GET HOLD OF PEPE AND TAKE HIM BACK TO GAUL.

41

FISH? YOU MUST BE OFF YOUR ROCKER! WHERE DO YOU THINK I'M GOING TO GET FISH AT THIS TIME OF NIGHT?

WHAT ARE YOU DOING WITH THE MAGIC POTION?

DOGMATIX! BREATHE! KEEP YOUR NOSE OUT OF THIS!

STOP THIEF!

38A

SCHLANG!

BRONTOSAURUS! WHAT ARE YOU DOING HERE IN CIVVIES?

THE DOPE! THE DOPE!

INSULTING ME, ARE YOU? ME, YOUR OLD COMRADE IN ARMS?

THAT GAUL! DON'T LET HIM GET THE DOPE!

HMM... THIS IS AS CLEAR AS MUD! LET'S GO AND SEE THE COMMANDER-IN-CHIEF.

38B

46

THE
END